BEN'S ULTRA-SECRET FILES

by Eric Luper

An Imprint of Penguin
Random House

CARTOON NETWORK BOOKS
Penguin Young Readers Group
An Imprint of Penguin Random House LLC

TM and © Cartoon Network. (s17). All rights reserved. Published in 2017 by
Cartoon Network Books, an imprint of Penguin Random House LLC,
345 Hudson Street, New York, New York 10014.
Manufactured in China.

ISBN 9780515159257   10 9 8 7 6 5 4 3 2 1

Yawn!
Boring page!

2

I don't know, Ben. There's a lot of important information over there. Publishing company. Addresses. Even a cute penguin!

Stop raining on my boring parade, Gwen. Now, where was I?

You were yawning.

NAME

One of the reasons I love computers is because they are so accurate!

RACE
Human

PLANET OF ORIGIN
Earth

DISTINGUISHING CHARACTERISTICS
Dreamy green eyes

APPEARANCE
» 10 years old
» Massive biceps

SPECIAL POWER[S]
The Omnitrix

ATTRIBUTES
Luscious brown hair

BEN TENNYSON

Winning smile

Wait a second. Who wrote these files?

Amazing sense of humor

Stylish clothing

I did, of course!

Fresh kicks

Well, your facts need a little tweaking.

NAME

Hey! The only thing you didn't change in the computer was about the Omnitrix.

RACE
Weirdo

PLANET OF ORIGIN
Who knows?

DISTINGUISHING CHARACTERISTICS
Moldy pea-soup-colored eyes

APPEARANCE
» 10 years old
» Twig-like arms

It's the only thing you got right.

SPECIAL POWER[S]
The Omnitrix

ATTRIBUTES
Messy mop atop meatball head

NAME

THE OMNITRIX

Adjustable wristband: Once a user puts it on, the Omnitrix cannot be removed.

Face plate: Slap it to turn into an alien.

FroYo maker

Wait, the Omnitrix makes frozen yogurt?

No, but it sounds way cooler!

Let's move on to some aliens.

NAME

RACE
Arburian Pelarota

PLANET OF ORIGIN
Arburia

COLOR[S]
Black, white, and yellow

SPECIAL POWER[S]
» Armadillo roll
» Super strength

ATTRIBUTES
» Enhanced endurance
» Enhanced speed
» Mega-tough

WEAKNESS[ES]
Kind of heavy

NAME

I'm lean, mean, and green!

RACE
Petrosapien

And not too keen.

PLANET OF ORIGIN
Petropia

COLOR[S]
Green

SPECIAL POWER[S]
» Shoots crystals
» Forms limbs into weapons
» Energy/laser blast reflection

ATTRIBUTES
» Super strength
» Enhanced durability

WEAKNESS[ES]
Can crack/shatter

DIAMONDHEAD

Pointy head

Ben, I'd watch who you call pointy-headed.

Massive forearms

Hard crystal limbs

Jagged edges

Skin is for the weak!

Skintight unisuit

18

Time for bed, you two. It's already thirteen in the morning!

Grandpa, there is no thirteen in the morning.

You both stay up so late, they had to add an extra hour!

NAME

Hex looks so weird.

RACE
Human

PLANET OF ORIGIN
Earth (probably someplace creepy)

You know, Ben, you really shouldn't make fun of how someone looks.

DISTINGUISHING CHARACTERISTIC[S]
» Tattoos on shoulders
» Black-and-white face paint
» Black nail polish on fingers and toes

APPEARANCE
» Shirtless, but with a stringy cape/hood thing
» Kickboxing foot wraps

SPECIAL POWER[S]
Magic

Gwen, the man walks around barefoot! With all those spells, don't you think he could conjure up some shoes?

SPECIAL ITEMS
» Spell books
» Staff
» Charms

Face paint looks like a bunch of dominoes

Manly chest

Nifty medallion

Hood protects from wind and rain

Tattered pants

Come on. Tattered pants? No shoes?

Gray toes

All right, now that you've pointed it out, the bare toes do sort of creep me out.

REAL NAME
Herbert J. Zomboni

Uh, uh, Gwen, you'd better take this one Clowns freak me out!

RACE
Human

How could a clown...? Ew... you're right. I'm freaked out, too!

PLANET OF ORIGIN
Earth

DISTINGUISHING CHARACTERISTIC[S]
He's a creepy clown!

APPEARANCE
Creepy clown!!

SPECIAL POWER[S]
Clever wordplay

SPECIAL ITEMS
» Tiny clown car
» Attack unicycle
» Banana peels
» Knockout gas
» Clown missile
» Giant vacuum cleaner

ZOMBOZO

Zany top hat

Wispy red hair

Razor-sharp teeth

Bright lipstick

Reflective armbands

Ringmaster-style tuxedo

Eek! Click off this page! Click off this page!

Pouf-y pants

All right, enough of that creepiness. Time to have a look at the heart and soul of my operation.
The refrigerator?
No, the Rust Bucket!
But Grandpa Max is sleeping in there.
He sleeps like the dead. Can't you hear him snoring?
I thought that was someone at another campsite cutting firewood with a chainsaw.

Storage rack/ jungle gym

High-powered LED lamps

Ben, the Rust Bucket is not a playground!

Why DOES our vehicle look like a garbage truck?

All-terrain tires

RUST BUCKET

Satellite dish

Rugged dump-truck hull

When was the last time you picked up your dirty socks?

Point taken!

Ladder for climbing

Alien UFO logo

NAME

ALIAS
Dr. Animo

RACE
Human

PLANET OF ORIGIN
Earth

OCCUPATION[S]
» Mad scientist
» Geneticist
» Veterinarian

> Dr. Animo needs some serious obedience training.

DISTINGUISHING CHARACTERISTIC[S]
Completely unhinged

SPECIAL POWER[S]
» Genetic genius
» Can manipulate DNA

ATTRIBUTES
So very old

WEAKNESS[ES]
Extremely focused on revenge

ALOYSIUS JAMES ANIMO

Male pattern baldness

Mullet hairstyle

Business in the front, psycho in the back.

DNA tanks

Sleeveless to show off . . . to show off what?

More random equipment

Ani-merger ray gun

My genius will not be stopped by a child with a fancy wristwatch, Ben Tennyson!

Did I mention you need obedience training?

Wait, is Dr. Animo behind the Ground Hawgs?

Whoever is behind this rodent problem doesn't know there's an exterminator in the house!

Spiky helmet

Flame-spitting exhaust pipes

Bikes by Ani-Motors

Skull belt buckle

GROUND HAWGS!!!

But what are they?

Various leather accessories

Bucktooth frown

Giant gophers, chipmunks, gerbils, marmots... whatever!

Spiky tires

NAME

RACE
Human

PLANET OF ORIGIN
Earth, probably France, probably southern France

Evil racecar driver is an occupation?

OCCUPATION
Evil racecar driver

It is now...

DISTINGUISHING CHARACTERISTIC[S]
Windswept hair

SPECIAL POWER[S]
» Lightning reflexes
» Mechanical gadgetry

ATTRIBUTES
Handsome and debonair

WEAKNESS[ES]
Road rage!!

Be a good little loser and go away!

LaGRANGE

SPECIAL WEAPONRY

- » Missiles
- » Land mines
- » Ice blast
- » Oil slick
- » Crushing tires
- » Windshield wipers

How are windshield wipers weapons?

Zey are not, but zey do come in handy in ze rain.

NAME

RACE
Cartoon

HEIGHT
Approximately 2 feet tall

You're as boring as an old folks' home at midnight!

PLACE OF ORIGIN
Ben's television

OCCUPATION
Zany cartoon superstar

Well, you're as boring as...as a...

Give it up, Ben.

DISTINGUISHING CHARACTERISTIC[S]
» He's a cartoon fox!   » Giggles a lot

SPECIAL POWER[S]
Only limited to his zany imagination

ATTRIBUTES
» Full of energy   » Bounces around

WEAKNESS[ES]
Prone to being struck by lightning

SPECIAL WEAPONRY
» Anvils   » Tar and feathering
» Bombs   » Paint

Unmatched power of imagination

Sometimes campfire songs are better than the zombie box.

Watch what you say about my beloved TV!

Beady yellow eyes

Fox tail

Mime gloves

Lavender fur

Red woolly sweater

 LET'S GET XINGY!!!

NAME

RACE
Human

Okay! Let's see what the computer has to say about you, Gwen!

PLANET OF ORIGIN
Earth

DISTINGUISHING CHARACTERISTIC[S]
» Always on the cutting edge of fashion
» Red hair

You wear a cat T-shirt.

SPECIAL POWER[S]
Can hike with the best of 'em!

ATTRIBUTES
» Spry
» Clever
» Good under pressure

WEAKNESS[ES]
Easily starstruck by teen heartthrobs

That's only once in a while!!

GWEN TENNYSON

Barrette

Halitosis

I don't have bad breath!

Flippy hair

Stylish cat

Your pet puppy agrees with me.

Long sleeves under short sleeves

Beanpole legs

I don't have a pet puppy, Ben.

Because he ran away from your halitosis!

NAME

Gah! I am the cat's pajamas!

My generation created *Titanics* and *Hindenburgs*! What do YOU have worth fighting for?

RACE
Human

SPECIAL POWER[S]
» Tinkering
» Very gentlemanly

ABILITIES
» Good at pulling levers
» Inventing

WEAKNESS[ES]
» Quick to anger
» Slave to etiquette
» Bigot

OTHER DETAILS
» Too much eyeliner
» Levers don't always work!

Plenty. Video games, camera phones, computer tablets, Wi-Fi!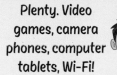

Steam-pipe hat

Brass epaulets

Muttonchops

Multiple pocket watches

Casually crossed leg

 Gah! I demand satisfaction!

VEHICLE NAME

OWNER
Steam Smythe

Squid! I hate squid!

It's a Clocktopus, not a squid, silly.

STYLE
Steampunk mech

APPEARANCE
Giant octopus

I hate Clocktopuses, too!

SPECIAL WEAPONRY
Tentacles for gripping and whacking

DEFENSE
» Flailing tentacles
» Can sink into water to lie in wait
» Steam Smythe's sharp words and witty banter

WEAKNESS(ES)
» Levers and pulleys don't always work!
» Water can douse furnace flames

CLOCKTOPUS

Steaminess

Steam pipes

Properly set clock

Bulbous furnaces of iron

Steel tentacles

Also, Four Arms can pluck off the tentacles one by one!

Gah! I demand satisfaction twice-ly!

The only satisfaction you'll get is escaping on your ornithopter!

DEFINITION
Ornithopter—a human-powered device that flies by flapping wings

NAME

Ooh, I do believe it's story time!

RACE
Human

SPECIAL POWER(S)
» Excellent manners
» Proper English
» Brilliant scientific notations

ABILITIES
Can turn anyone into a baby

WEAKNESS(ES)
Easily enraged by poor manners

GADGETS
» Handcuff highchairs
» Baby powder superweapon
[to turn whole cities into babies!]
» Knuckle ruler
» Nanny umbrella

Buuuurrrppp!

Repugnant! Stop that this instant!

NANNY NIGHTMARE

Flippy hair (with way too much hairspray)

Upturned nose

Purple/magenta eye shadow

Too much lipstick

Sharp nails

Black apron (to match her dark heart)

NANNY'S UMBRELLA
» Puffs out baby powder
» Shoots candy
» Helps Nanny fly

(OLD) NANNY NIGHTMARE

Wrinkles

Bad back

Gray hair

Wrinkles have wrinkles

I feel kind of bad that Nanny Nightmare got so old.

Bum knee

When I get my hands on you, I'll swat some manners into you both!

On second thought . . .

NAME

ALIAS(ES)

Boy, is that guy full of himself.

» Guardian?
» Protector!!

Well, isn't that the pot calling the kettle black?

RACE

Human

SPECIAL POWERS

Hubris

Pots? Kettles? Are you making mac and cheese for me, Gwen?

ABILITIES

Creating his own disasters to "save the day"

SPECIAL WEAPONRY

» Panamanian poison frog blow darts
» Antivenom
» Hypno-totem
» Ninja smoke vial
» Belt buckle rope/winch
» Retractable wingsuit
» Flask of Tasmanian tar pit
» Webbing of Sumatran king spider
» Bermudan serpent saliva

NAME

RACE
Tetramand

PLANET OF ORIGIN
Khoros

COLOR[S]
Red with black-and-white suit

DISTINGUISHING CHARACTERISTIC[S]
» Four arms
» Four eyes

SPECIAL POWER[S]
» Super strength
» Mega-jump
» Sonic clap

ATTRIBUTES
» Super durable
» Deep, manly voice

WEAKNESS[ES]
Somewhat slow

Who are you calling "slow?"

FOUR ARMS

Massive arms

Protruding jaw

Forearm spines

Punching solves my problems!

Wrecking-ball fists

Double the armpits

All the better to make gross sounds with!!

I prefer Baby Four Arms.

Goo goo!

NAME

RACE
Galvan

PLANET OF ORIGIN
Galvan Prime

COLOR[S]
Grey with green suit

DISTINGUISHING CHARACTERISTIC[S]
» Froglike appearance
» Orange eyes

SPECIAL POWER[S]
» Unmatched intelligence
» Can create gadgets from spare parts
» Wall climbing

ATTRIBUTES
» Tiny
» Grabby frog tongue

WEAKNESS[ES]
Not physically durable

Who needs strength when superior intellect can effectively change the trajectory of a conflict to my advantage?

Disproportionately large cranium

What's a cranium?

It's a head.

See, even the computer knows I'm clever.

Clever smile

Sticky fingers

One-tenth clever. I'll give you that.

I'll take it!!

Sticky toes

NAME

RACE
Pyronite

PLACE OF ORIGIN
Pyros

COLOR[S]
Red with yellow cracks

DISTINGUISHING CHARACTERISTIC[S]
» Flaming head
» Exudes heat

SPECIAL POWER[S]
» Fireballs
» Flaming punches
» Flight

ATTRIBUTES
» Magnetic personality
» Devastating good looks

WEAKNESS[ES]
Exposure to water
extinguishes flames

Fireballs

Flaming head

You also forgot to mention that I can burp flames.

Magma body

Aura of heat

And that you can make popcorn in about two seconds!

Flame-wisp toes

NAME

RACE
Florauna

PLANET OF ORIGIN
Flors Verdance

COLOR[S]
Green, green, and green

DISTINGUISHING CHARACTERISTIC[S]
» Vine-y limbs
» Single eye

SPECIAL POWER[S]
» Plant control
» Rapid growth
» Explosive seeds
» Fast tunneling
» Regeneration

ATTRIBUTES
» Very vine-y
» Thorny fingers

WEAKNESS[ES]
» Probably weed killer
» Can be clumsy
» Can get tangled

WILDVINE

Uni-eye

Uni-brow

Seed pods

Leafy collar

Sprouts

Vine-y limbs

My collar is the height of Florauna fashion!

Somebody get me a hedge clipper and a rake.

NAME

OWNER
Dr. Animo

Tail for striking

Gallons of digestive acid

Ten legs

NAME LORD DECIBEL

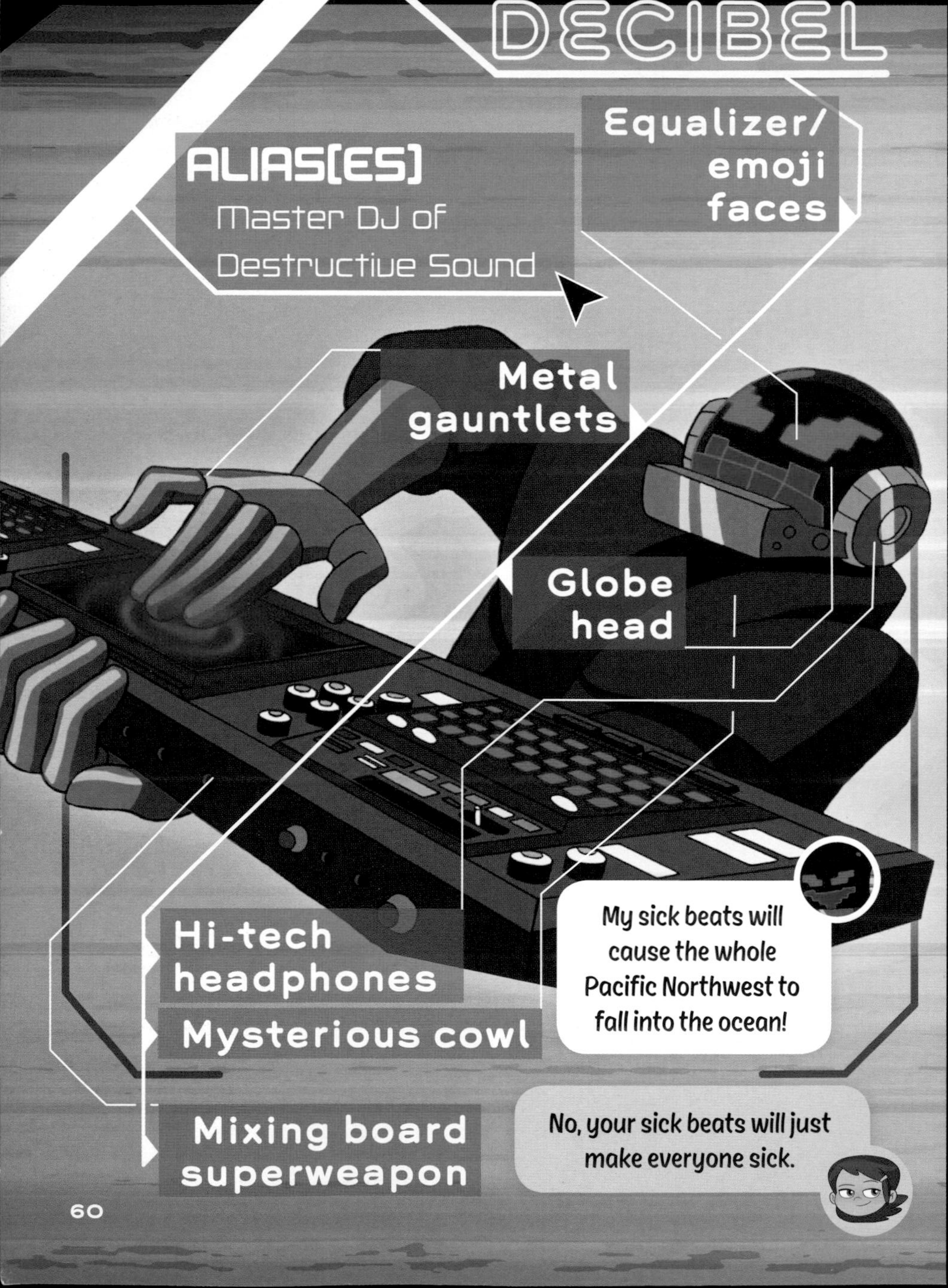

Enough bad guys! Time for Lucky Girl to save the day. I helped defeat Hex!

You were just lucky.

Nifty mask

Nifty digital watch

Exactly! That's why they call me **Lucky Girl**.

Nifty cape

Why is everything about you labeled **nifty**?

Because everything about Lucky Girl is nifty!

Everything about Lucky Girl is coincidence.

NAME — **MAURICE**

RACE
Bug Man

HOBBIES
Collecting waste to power Maggonet

ABILITIES
Brilliant scientist

WEAKNESS(ES)
» Only six inches tall
» Yells often

Slick hair

Beady eyes

Tiny pincers

Pencil-thin mustache

Six legs

I will use my mighty Maggonet to create a maggot monster who will swallow all of Las Vegas!

Sounds like a complicated plan, little bug man.

NAME **SIDNEY**

RACE
Bug Man

HOBBIES
Following Maurice's orders

SKILLS
» Brawny
» Barfs slime

WEAKNESS[ES]
» Can't talk
» Not so smart

Antennae

Radiation
suit

Rrrawwwwrrrr!!!!

You took the words
right out of my
mouth.

Sleevelessness
(to show off
massive guns)

Protective
rubber
gloves

This campsite is so dirty, I'd have to turn into Four Arms to move the Rust Bucket, Heatblast to sanitize the area, Overflow to rinse everything off, Cannonbolt to smooth everything out, and Grey Matter to figure out how to do it all without waking everyone up.

Don't you dare.

But I wanna, Gwen!

Let's look at some alien heroes instead.

NAME

RACE
Orishan

PLANET OF ORIGIN
Kiusana

COLOR[S]
Red with blue water tanks

DISTINGUISHING CHARACTERISTIC[S]
Water pipes across chest

SPECIAL POWER[S]
» Hydro-blast
» Limited flight with water jets

ATTRIBUTES
» Armored exoskeleton
» Durable

WEAKNESS[ES]
Unknown

That's right, no known weaknesses.

Is being annoying a weakness?

I'd consider it a strength!

NAME

RACE
Lepidopterran

PLANET OF ORIGIN
Lepidopterra

COLOR[S]
Blue with yellow wings

DISTINGUISHING CHARACTERISTIC[S]
Uh . . . wings?

SPECIAL POWER[S]
» Agile flight
» Stinky gas
» Slime bolts

I'm not sure Stinkfly smells any worse than your two-week-used underwear.

ATTRIBUTES
» 360-degree vision
» Extremely smelly

I propose an experiment, Gwen. You can be the subject!

WEAKNESS[ES]
» Fragile wings
» Unable to swim
» Can gas himself!

STINKFLY

Antennae

Pearly white teeth

Insectoid wings

Slime ports

Slender body

Chitin exoskeleton

What is **chitin**?

It's what bugs are made of.

I thought they were made of awesomeness!

NAME

RACE
Kineceleran

PLANET OF ORIGIN
Kinet

COLOR[S]
Black and blue

I'll leave YOU black and blue!

DISTINGUISHING CHARACTERISTIC[S]
Looks a little like a velociraptor

SPECIAL POWER[S]
» Super speed
» Insane agility
» Sharp claws

ATTRIBUTES
Aerodynamic

WEAKNESS[ES]
Does not run well on ice

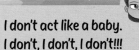

NAME

RACE
Galvanic Mechamorph

PLANET OF ORIGIN
Galvan B (Galvan Prime's Moon)

COLOR(S)
Indigo and violet

Couldn't they just say purple and purple?

DISTINGUISHING CHARACTERISTIC(S)
» Very purply
» Fluid-like body

SPECIAL POWER(S)
» Can control and upgrade technology
» Optic beam

ATTRIBUTES
» Can change body shape
» Increased strength
» Increased flexibility

WEAKNESS(ES)
» Electricity
» Electromagnetic pulse

Gelatinous body

Smush-y head

Stretchy limbs

External circuitry

Indigo

Violet

 Purple and purple!!

Shhh, Ben, you'll wake up Grandpa Max.

But now you're tired. We were going to hike Mount Dirtytoe today. There's a cabin at the top where they have the world's largest mouse skull on display.

Sounds like fun.

Yeah, we're totally up for doing that, Grandpa Max. But first, let's see what the computer has to say about you.

NAME

RACE
Human

PLANET OF ORIGIN
Earth

DISTINGUISHING CHARACTERISTIC[S]
» Debonair white streak
» Height of fine fashion
» Wrinkles

Wait a second.
You said you wouldn't
mention my wrinkles.

SPECIAL POWER[S]
» Excellent driver
» Master badminton player
» Handy, but can't always
fix the Rust Bucket

Now you're really
hitting below the belt.

ATTRIBUTES
» Organized enough to give Ben chores
» Could afford to lose a few pounds

WEAKNESS[ES]
Needs a lot of sleep

Your poor, poor belt . . .
Working so hard.

GRANDPA MAX

Silver hair

Neatly pressed crewneck T-shirt

Strapping arms

Neatly pressed Hawaiian shirt

Neatly pressed adventure vest

Gold retirement watch

Neatly pressed slacks

You'll both regret not getting any sleep when we're twelve miles into our hike.

Oh no! It's a Hydromander! He's destroying the whole campground!

Raaawwrrr!!!